Stone Soup

Retold by Marilyn Sapienza • Illustrations by Hans Wilhelm

Weekly Reader Books
Middletown, Connecticut

Weekly Reader Books offers several exciting
card and activity programs. For information,
write to WEEKLY READER BOOKS, P.O. Box 16636,
Columbus, Ohio 43216.

This book is a presentation of Weekly Reader Books. Weekly Reader
Books offers book clubs for children from preschool through high
school. For further information write to: **Weekly Reader Books,**
4343 Equity Drive, Columbus, Ohio 43228.

Stone Soup

"I'M tired. I'm hungry," whined Molly.

"Don't worry," said Max. "Our troubles are over. Look! I see a little village just a few miles away."

"But we don't know anyone there," said Molly.

Max thought for a moment. "Hmmm," he said. "You're right. But maybe some friendly villagers live there. Maybe they'll give us something to eat and a place to rest."

"Yes," said Molly. "Most people are kind. Let's go."

What Molly and Max didn't know is that *these* villagers weren't kind. They were stingy and mean.

"EEEEK!" shouted Mr. and Mrs. Ratfink. "Eeeek!" shrieked their little baby too.

"Strangers are coming!" yelled Mr. Ratfink. "They'll want us to share what we have with them."

"Eeek!" squealed Baby Ratfink.

"Let's hide our food. Let's close our shops," said the butcher.

The town banker hid his money. He put a sign on the bank: "CLOSED."

The village innkeeper hid his room keys. He put a sign on the hotel: "NO ROOM."

The farmer's wife hid the garden vegetables. She closed the door and shuttered the windows.

The townspeople hid carrots and corn. They hid potatoes and peas. They hid beans and broccoli, onions and herbs, milk and meat. Soon, there was not one bit of food in sight!

All the villagers practiced looking hungry.

But by the time Molly and Max reached the
village, there was no one around.

"Where is everyone?" asked Molly.

"They're probably inside having lunch," reasoned
Max. "Can't you smell something delicious?"

"Yes," said Molly. "It's coming from that house
over there. The door is even open a crack."

"Maybe they saw us coming and are waiting
for us," said Max hopefully.

But when Molly and Max got to the door, it
slammed shut. "Go away," shouted a voice from
behind the door.

Molly and Max walked up to a man who was
crossing the street.

"Excuse me, Sir," said Molly. "Could you
please help us. We've been traveling a long time.
We could use a hot meal. And a place to sleep."

"Forget it!" said the man in a gruff voice.

Molly and Max knocked on every door. They stopped everyone who passed by. But the answers were always the same. "No food." "No room." "Go away."

"What are we going to do?" asked Molly. "No one here can help us."

"I have a feeling that no one here *wants* to help us," said Max. "I think these people have hearts of stone."

"Hey," said Molly. "That gives me an idea!"

Molly whispered her idea to Max. Then they
rang the village bell. BONG! BONG! BONG!
went the bell. All the townspeople came running.

"What's going on here," grumbled Mr. Ratfink. "We only ring the bell when there's an emergency."

"Eeeek!" screeched Baby Ratfink.

"There is an emergency," Max told everyone. "There's no food in this town."

"So now is the time to make Stone Soup," said Molly.

"Stone Soup? I've never heard of it," said the farmer's wife.

"Of course you haven't heard of it," said Molly. "It's a secret recipe."

"But we'll share the recipe with you just the same," said Max. "Then we'll all have something to eat and none of us will be hungry."

"Well," said the villagers impatiently, "what do we do first?"

Molly answered, "*Heat some water in a pot.*"

When that was done, the villagers said,
"What's next?"

Max answered, "*Add some stones you've
scrubbed a lot.*"

Now the townspeople were really curious.
Surely this was the strangest recipe they
had ever heard.

They waited while Molly dipped her spoon into
the steaming pot. They watched while she tasted
the soup.

"Mmmm," she said. "Stone Soup is very good plain.
But it would taste even better if we could make
the fancy kind."

"How do we do that?" asked the Mayor.

"*Sprinkle pepper, salt, and herbs,*" said Molly.
"*Let it boil undisturbed.*"

"I have those things," said the Mayor's wife.
"I'll be right back."

She hurried back with her pocket full
of herbs and spices.

"Oh, thank you," said Molly, as she added the
seasonings to the soup.

"What's next?" asked the Mayor's wife.

"*Drop in carrots, onions too.
Let the soup heat through and
through,*" said Molly. "But we'll
just have to do without carrots
and onions," she sighed.

"I have those things," said
the farmer's wife. "I'll be
right back."

She came back with a sack bulging with carrots and onions.

"Oh, thank you," said Molly, as she added them to the soup.

"What's next?" asked the farmer's wife.

Molly replied, "*Stir in milk to make it sweet. Add potatoes for a treat.* With milk and potatoes it would be so much better."

"I have milk," shouted the butcher's wife. "And the banker's wife has potatoes. We'll be right back."

The butcher's wife returned with two buckets brimming with milk. The banker's wife came back with a basket full of potatoes.

"Oh, thank you," said Molly as she added them to the soup.

"What's next?" asked the banker's wife.

Max replied, "*Toss in meat cubes.
Let it stew. Let it bubble.
Let it brew.*"

"Too bad we don't have any
meat," sighed Molly.

"I know where to get some,"
said the butcher excitedly.
"I'll be right back."

A short time later, the butcher
returned with a huge chunk of
meat which he quickly cut into
pieces.

"Oh, thank you," said Molly
as she stirred the meat pieces into
the boiling pot.

"What's next?" asked the butcher.

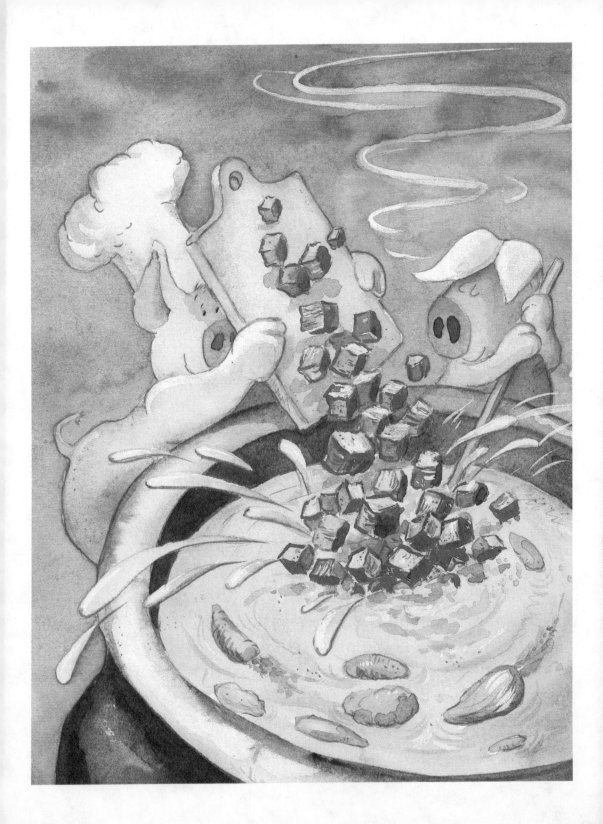

"The best part," said Molly. "*Taste the soup and when it's done, serve Stone Soup to everyone.*"

"Yay!" cheered the Mayor. "It's time to taste the soup." He snatched up a spoonful of soup and tasted it. "This is the most delicious soup I've ever had!" said the Mayor. "And to think that it's made with nothing but stones and water. Amazing!"

"It's time to serve the Stone Soup," announced the Mayor. But the townspeople had more than just soup. They also had fruit and bread, salad and cider, cakes and pies. They ate and laughed and danced long into the night. And when the feast was over, the innkeeper asked Molly and Max to stay in his finest room.

The next morning, everyone waved good-bye to Molly and Max. "How can we thank you for the secret recipe?" they called.

"Share Stone Soup with everyone," sang the travelers.

RECIPE FOR STONE SOUP

Heat some water in a pot.
Add some stones you've scrubbed a lot.

Sprinkle pepper, salt, and herbs.
Let it boil undisturbed.

Drop in carrots, onions too.
Let the soup heat through and through.

Stir in milk to make it sweet.
Add potatoes for a treat.

Toss in meat cubes. Let it stew.
Let it bubble. Let it brew.

Taste the soup and when it's done,
Share Stone Soup with everyone.